This Book Belongs To:

CONTENTS

John Harrold.

ISBN 0-85079-159-6

RUPERT

John Harrold.

£2·95

RUPERT and the

*While hunting windfalls one fine day
Rupert hears someone calling, "Hey!"*

"**H**ey, Rupert!" Rupert who has been searching the orchard for windfall apples this fine autumn day, turns to find Willie Mouse. "Bill Badger has called a meeting on the common and he wants you to come," Willie announces. He doesn't know what the meeting is about, but Rupert is not having much luck with apples so he is glad to go. On the common they find the others deep in conversation. "I've got a good idea," is how Bill Badger

Strange Airman

"Bill's called the pals and wants you there,"
Says Willie Mouse. So off they tear.

Bill's plan is – it is soon made clear –
To have one huge bonfire out here.

greets Rupert. "Instead of separate bonfires and fireworks on Guy Fawkes night as usual, let's have one super bonfire out here on the common." "That's a great idea!" cries Rupert. "Yes, we all think so!" Algy Pug chimes in. "Then let's start collecting wood for it right away," says Rupert. So the friends scatter to collect bonfire fuel and soon Rupert finds he is working with Willie on the edge of the woods. Neither hears a big car pull up near them.

They all agree Bill's idea's good
And so set off to gather wood.

A car pulls up, two men get out.
Thinks Rupert, "What's this all about?"

They're looking for a boy, they say,
Named Alaric who lives this way.

But Rupert tells them, "I don't know
Of such a boy. Now we must go."

He hurries back in some alarm.
He's sure those men mean someone harm.

Rupert and Willie are starting back with their bundles when two foreign-looking men get out of the car and start towards them. Rupert doesn't much like the look of them. And he doesn't like the sound of the taller one who blocks his path and demands curtly, "The boy Alaric – you must know him – he is somewhere in these parts. It is urgent that we find him." Rupert gulps. "I–I've never heard of any boy called Alaric," he quavers. The men look as if they find this hard to believe but they say no more and stand aside to let Rupert and Willie scurry gratefully away.

As soon as they reach the spot where the super bonfire is to be built Rupert grabs Bill. "Do *you* know anyone called Alaric?" he asks then pours out the story of the two strangers. "Never heard of anyone called Alaric," Bill says. "Funny sort of name, anyway. But I shouldn't worry about it. Now let's get on with building the bonfire." Rupert, though, still feels uneasy about the strangers.

RUPERT GETS THE GUY

But Bill says, "Rupert, do please try
To worry less and find a guy."

And so to Farmer Grimes he goes
And asks for one of his scarecrows.

Against the pile some steps they prop
And Rupert sticks the guy on top.

Then when it's dark they light their fire,
And dancing, watch the flames leap higher.

The bonfire pile grows rapidly. But Rupert can't forget the two men and their search for Alaric. Whoever Alaric is, Rupert feels sure that the men mean him harm. At length Bill Badger cries, "For goodness sake, Rupert, stop worrying! Go and find something that will do for a guy. Maybe Farmer Grimes will let us have a scarecrow."

In fact, Farmer Grimes is an old friend and when Rupert finds him and explains what's wanted he is only too happy to help.

Rupert is so delighted with the scarecrow-guy that he forgets his earlier worries and carries his trophy proudly back to the chums. A ladder is found and he is given the honour of climbing to the top of the bonfire pile and fixing the guy in place there.

That evening when it is dark the bonfire is lit. It's the best bonfire the chums have seen, and as they dance around it Rupert is as carefree as the rest. Suddenly there is a roar from the sky!

A sudden roaring noise they hear.
A 'plane's in trouble somewhere near.

"Look out!" they cry. "It's going to smash
Into those trees . . . Oh, what a crash!"

They clamber on the crumpled 'plane,
But, for the pilot, look in vain.

The noise has brought out Mr. Bear.
They search some more, but no one's there.

The roaring gets louder and louder. The chums cluster together in alarm as it seems to come right over their heads. Then Bill points. "Look! It's an aircraft!" he shouts. "The pilot must be in trouble!" cries Rupert. "Maybe the light from our bonfire brought him here." They can all see the machine now, caught in the glow from the flames. "Look out!" Bill gasps. "He's going to hit the edge of the woods if he's not careful." And to the chums' horror, that's what happens.

Rupert and the others rush to where the 'plane hit. Rupert clambers on to the crumpled wing to look into the cockpit. It is empty! The pilot must have been thrown out when the machine crashed, Bill suggests. But though they search as best they can, the chums can find no trace of anyone. Even when Rupert's Daddy who has heard the crash, turns up with a lamp they have no better luck. "Then the pilot must have parachuted out before his 'plane got here," decides Mr. Bear.

RUPERT SEARCHES AGAIN

They think the man has baled out so
They stop the search and home they go.

But Rupert still feels that he should
Get up at dawn and search the wood.

So up he gets at break of day
And to the crashed 'plane makes his way

Near there a parachute he sees,
Caught with a man, high in the trees.

Unhappily the chums decide that they must give
up the search and Mr. Bear takes Rupert home.
When Mrs. Bear hears what the noise was all about
she throws up her hands and cries, "It's a mercy
that thing didn't fall on the lot of you!" But Rupert
is still worrying about the missing pilot as he gets
ready for bed. "I know!" he decides. "I'll get up
very early and have another search." So he takes
his alarm clock and sets it to call him at daybreak.
Then he climbs into bed.

It is hardly light when the jangle of the alarm
wakens Rupert. He gets up, dresses and sets off
through the cold air for the woods and the spot
where the 'plane crashed. He starts his search
there moving away from it in widening circles. But
still he can find no trace of the pilot. Then out of
the corner of his eye he sees a movement high in
the branches of a tree. Something is tangled in
those branches. And hanging from it is what looks
like a man!

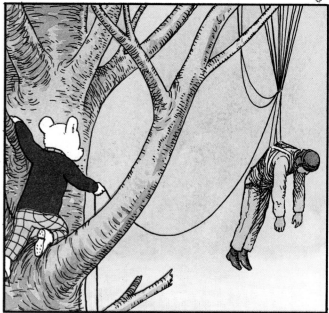

The man's unconscious, that's soon plain,
For Rupert calls to him in vain.

So up he climbs among the boughs
And tries – no luck! – the man to rouse.

"The cord is strong," he thinks. "I'll see
If I can pull him on the tree.

He props him up as best he can.
"Must reach Alaric," groans the man.

"Daddy was right!" Rupert tells himself. "The pilot *did* parachute out of his 'plane. But closer to us than we thought." He dashes across to the tree where the pilot is hanging. He calls out to the man but there is no answer. Then he sees that a broken cord from the parachute is hanging down. He takes this and scrambles up the tree until he is opposite the pilot. Gently he tugs the cord. There is no sign of life from the man. But Rupert does find that he can pull the man quite easily towards himself. "Well, I can't just leave him hanging there," he decides and starts to pull the pilot slowly closer and closer. A couple of times he almost tumbles out of the tree with the effort, but finally he manages to prop the airman safely in the branches. To his joy the man is breathing and he seems to be murmuring something. Rupert bends close. He can scarcely believe his ears. For the man is mumbling, "Alaric, I must get to Alaric." That name again!

RUPERT FETCHES HELP

He runs for help and Nutwood-bound
Meets Bill and tells him what he's found.

Then Mr. Bear turns up to say,
"We must get him down right away."

He sends the two pals up to see
If they can get the man's 'chute free.

Then round a branch the cords are wound
To lower the airman to the ground.

Rupert ropes the airman so that he can't fall then scrambles down from the tree and races for help. The first person he sees is Bill who, like Rupert himself, has decided to make another search. "I've found the pilot!" pants Rupert. "And guess what! He's asking for someone called Alaric!" "You've got Alaric on the brain!" Bill says, but he presses on to see for himself while Rupert runs home to fetch Mr. Bear. When Mr. Bear sees the pilot he says, "We must get him down at once!"

He climbs up beside the unconscious pilot then sends Rupert and Bill, who are first-class climbers, higher still to untangle the parachute. It is hard work but they manage it and Mr. Bear who meanwhile has cut off more of its cords, is able to lower the airman over a strong bough gently to the ground.

"No time to lose now," says Mr. Bear briskly. "We must get him home and see how badly he is injured. You pair fetch two poles to make a stretcher."

RUPERT MAKES AN OFFER

Then, on a makeshift stretcher laid,
The airman's taken for first aid.

He's told, when he's tucked up in bed,
He broke his arm and struck his head.

Says Rupert, "Since you are too sick
To go, let me fetch Alaric."

The man says, "Yes, but you must show
That ring and then he'll come, I know.

With the poles Rupert and Bill fetch and the parachute Mr. Bear makes a stretcher. Then they carry the airman to Rupert's cottage where Dr. Lion is called. He finds that the man has a broken arm and must have struck his head on a branch. Slowly the man comes round. "Where am I?" he whispers. "I must get to . . ." "There is nothing to worry about," says Dr. Lion. But Rupert knows there must be, and who it is the airman wants to reach so badly. So, as soon as Dr. Lion has gone, he steals into the bedroom. "Earlier you spoke of Alaric," he says softly to the man. "Who is he?" "That I cannot tell you," the man breathes. "But he is in great danger and now I cannot reach him." Then Rupert has an idea. "But can't I go and bring him here to you?" he asks. The man looks at him for a moment then says, "Yes, it is the only chance. Show him the ring you will find in the inside pocket of my tunic and he will come with you." Rupert feels in the pocket and finds the ring.

RUPERT ASKS A CROW THE WAY

"Where is the boy?" The man replies,
"The Old Red Grange. Watch out for spies!"

Then Rupert meets a wise old crow
And asks the way that he should go.

"The Old Red Grange," the bird replies,
"Behind that distant hill-top lies."

"To walk so far, you've not a hope!
But I can help. Just fetch some rope."

"Alaric," the airman tells Rupert, "is living in hiding at a place called the Old Red Grange. But hurry and be careful for there are spies seeking him to do him harm." "Spies!" Rupert repeats. "Then that's what those men were!" And he tells of the two men who questioned him about Alaric. The airman looks even more anxious. "Then you must not waste a moment," he urges. So off Rupert goes wondering how to get to the Old Red Grange. And on a gate he spots someone who might just know.

It is a wise old crow who flies everywhere, sees everything and has helped Rupert before. The crow gets Rupert to climb a nearby tree and joins him there. "Beyond that distant hill lies the Old Red Grange," it croaks. "It's much too far for you to walk." "But I must get to it!" Rupert protests. "There's a boy in great danger there." "In that case I'll see what I can do," the crow says. "You go and fetch some rope." "Rope?" Rupert puzzles. Then he remembers the parachute cords.

13

RUPERT GOES BY CROW

*The parachute cord's just the thing
To make a sort of bird-borne swing.*

*The crows each take a line and rise
With Rupert, to his great surprise.*

*They fly across the distant range
Of hills and reach the Old Red Grange.*

*A startled boy is close at hand
When Rupert Bear comes in to land.*

Rupert hurries to where the parachute cords were left, and while he is sorting them out the crow turns up with five of his family. "Tie three ropes together in the middle," the bird orders. Rupert does so. "Now sit on them," it adds. Very puzzled Rupert does as he's told. At once each of the six crows takes one end of a rope and soar upwards, taking a very astonished Rupert with them. Holding on for all he's worth, Rupert is soon sailing high over the treetops.

In no time at all the crows have carried Rupert over the distant hill, and there below is a fine old house. The crows swoop on it and deposit Rupert in the middle of a garden behind thick, high hedges. A boy is standing there, staring, half in astonishment, half in alarm at the arrival of this stranger from the sky. Then he seems to pull himself together. He takes a deep breath and says in a voice that is meant to sound stern "This garden is private. No one may come in."

RUPERT MEETS ALARIC

When Rupert shows the boy the ring
He cries, "It's owner is my king!"

He's Alaric, he says, and they
Must leave this place without delay.

His guardian agrees that he
Must find the airman and then flee.

The boy says, "Though my pony's swift,
It might be best to get a lift."

Rupert picks himself up. "Are you Alaric?" he asks. The boy looks startled. "How do you know that?" he demands. Rupert's answer is to produce the ring. The boy looks even more astonished. "How did you get that?" he marvels. "It belongs to the king of my own country." Now it is Rupert's turn to be astounded, but he pours out his story. "That airman must be a King's Messenger," declares the boy. "I must go to him. And you must lead me. Now come with me while I tell my guardian."

At Alaric's excited call an old gentleman appears on the terrace of the house. Gravely he hears what Alaric has to say. "Yes," he agrees, "that is the king's ring. You must go, Alaric." "Come!" Alaric tells Rupert. "My pony shall carry us to Nutwood. It is in the paddock across the road." But before the pair can cross the road they see a car approaching. "It might be much quicker by that car if they're going our way and would give us a lift," says Alaric. "Let's try."

RUPERT AND ALARIC FLEE

The car stops and two men get out.
The spies! "That's Alaric!" they shout.

"My pony!" cries the boy. They dash
Across the paddock in a flash.

They reach their mount. Are they too late?
The spies are charging through the gate.

But no! They're off and soon they find
They've left the villains far behind.

The car slows as Rupert and Alaric wave it down. It stops. The doors open. And to Rupert's horror, out climb the two strangers who questioned him in Nutwood. "Run, Alaric!" he shouts. "Those are the spies who are after you!" The two turn and dash into the paddock where Alaric's pony is kept. As they run Alaric pants, "I know that pair. They are enemies of my king and me!" By the time the pair reach the pony the men are coming through the gate. Alaric is plainly a good horseman for he springs on to the animal's bare back and pulls Rupert up behind him. Then with a whoop he races the pony out of the paddock's further gate. "Now if you guide me," he tells Rupert, "we'll make a bee-line over the hill where their car cannot possibly follow us.

The animal is fresh and sets a great pace even up steep slopes. And soon they are speeding over the crest of the hill. "Over there!" Rupert cries. "That village. That's Nutwood!"

They easily outrun the spies.
"And here's our cottage!" Rupert cries.

Out comes the airman, kneels before
Young Alaric outside the door.

The king, his uncle, it appears,
Feels he has reigned too many years.

"So now I'm king!" the young boy cries.
"And thanks to you I've slipped the spies."

To Rupert's great relief there is no sign of the two spies when Alaric and he reach his own cottage. "We've beaten them, Alaric!" he cries. At the sound of his voice the door opens and the airman steps out. Rupert is surprised to see him dressed in the uniform he was wearing under his flying kit. He still looks pretty weak. At the sight of Alaric he drops on one knee and addresses him in a language Rupert doesn't understand. "Who *is* this Alaric?" Rupert wonders. "What is he?"

Inside the cottage the airman gives Alaric a document to read. The boy studies it seriously. Then he notices Rupert's puzzled expression. "My little friend," he smiles, "we come from a far country. My uncle was king. He has decided he is too old to rule any longer and the people wish me to reign in his place. Thanks to you we have so far escaped those enemies who are plotting against me. But now this messenger and I must leave at once." "But how?" Rupert asks.

RUPERT AND THE CROWS HELP

They must leave now. They try the 'plane.
But it will never fly again.

His flight, it seems, the crows thought fun.
Cries Rupert, "Have another one!"

He runs to tell his friends his plan.
"They couldn't do it," says the man.

But Rupert says, "As one who knows,
I tell you, you can trust the crows."

"Perhaps my 'plane can be got to work," the airman suggests. "Of course, you haven't seen it since you crashed," Rupert says. "I know nothing about 'planes but it doesn't look to me as if it could be mended." And the airman has to agree when Rupert shows him the wreck. While they rack their brains for a way to escape, Rupert wanders off a little way to think. He jumps when a voice croaks, "That jaunt to the Old Red Grange was fun. We all enjoyed it." It is the wise crow.

That's it! "Come with me and you can have even more fun," Rupert tells the crow. "Bring as many of your friends and family as you can." And a few minutes later, followed by a flock of happily cawing crows, he is explaining his plan to Alaric and the airman. The airman doesn't think the crows can do it, but Rupert persuades him to let them try, and Alaric tells how the crows brought Rupert to fetch him. Then off dashes Rupert to get what is left of the parachute.

They fix the cords with lots of ends
And make a seat for Rupert's friends.

At last the crow-borne chair takes flight
While Rupert waves them out of sight.

Next day the crows return and bring
A gift for Rupert from the king.

It is – how proud his parents are! –
A lovely golden, jewelled star.

Using some of the parachute's silk and all the cord, Rupert and Alaric fashion a seat comfortable enough for the injured airman. They are careful to leave as many ends of cord free as they can. When they are done, the old crow croaks an order, the rest of the flock seize the cord ends, and up and away go Alaric and the airman soaring smoothly towards the coast. "Well, this is a much better end to that adventure than I expected," thinks Rupert as he waves them goodbye.

But the story isn't quite over. For next evening when Rupert is wandering on the common he sees a flock of birds flying out of the distance. It is the crows returning. He runs to greet them. To his surprise the old crow flies straight to him and drops a little packet into his hands.

Rupert dashes home to open it. And how everyone gasps! For inside is a golden star set with gems. And with it is a letter asking him to keep it in memory of how he once helped a king. The End.

RUPERT

*High on the common Rupert Bear
Is seeking Christmas holly there.*

Christmas is near. On Nutwood Common Rupert is after holly. He finds a splendid bush and is about to cut the first bunch when . . . "Rupert!" Someone calls him. He spins round and at first there seems to be no one there. Then from a clump of bushes behind him steps someone he knows – Santa Claus's messenger, the little cowboy. Before Rupert can speak the cowboy rushes on, "Santa needs your help badly! Look!" He tugs a pair of reins attached to

and **Rika**

*He finds a bush, is just about
To start work when he hears a shout.*

*"All Santa's reindeer can't be found.
Just one's come from their grazing ground."*

something in the bushes and out steps a reindeer. "This is the only reindeer Santa has. The others ain't come back from their holiday grazing grounds in Lapland. I'm too busy to go get them so Santa wants you to take this reindeer, Blitzen, and fetch the others. Blitzen knows the way. But with Christmas so near you'll have to go right now. I've got to get back pronto in my airplane." He waves at his little machine some way off.

*"We need your help to find the rest.
This one will take you. Do your best."*

John Harrold.

RUPERT GOES REINDEER RIDING

"I'll ask my Mummy," Rupert cries.
"Wait here for me." And home he flies

"Of course, you must help Santa, dear,"
Says Mrs. Bear. "Your duty's clear."

"You're heading for the land of Lapp.
In case you need it, take this map."

"In fact, this reindeer's sure to know
Those parts real well. So off you go!"

"I – I'll have to ask Mummy," stammers Rupert, quite taken aback. "Then go ask her now!" says the cowboy urgently. "And tell her Santa says that without reindeer he won't be able to bring round everyone's presents in time for Christmas." With no more ado Rupert dashes home and pours out to Mrs. Bear Santa's plea for help. "Well, dear," she says after a moment, "if it's as urgent as all that and you are going on a nice safe reindeer, then, yes, you may go." And she bundles him into his warmest coat. So back to the common Rupert races to find the cowboy waiting anxiously. "Great!" the cowboy exclaims when Rupert tells him that his Mummy has agreed. He hoists Rupert into the reindeer Blitzen's saddle. Then he hands up a map. "Blitzen should know the way," he says. "But take this just in case . . ." Now he leads Blitzen onto a rocky outcrop, tells Rupert to hold tight, then gives a wild whoop. With a mighty bound Blitzen launches itself and Rupert into the winter sky.

RUPERT REACHES SNOW LAND

From Nutwood skies they gallop forth,
Bound for the dark and frozen North.

The North at last! A lake with isles.
Dark trees and snow for miles and miles.

The reindeer hears a tinkling sound
And swiftly swoops towards the ground.

Against the moonlit stretch of snow
Some moving shapes begin to show.

Up, up goes Blitzen until Nutwood looks like a toy village far below. But the reindeer moves so smoothly that Rupert doesn't feel at all scared. In fact, he is rather enjoying himself and wonders if anyone below can see him. "If they can," he thinks, "they must be jolly curious about what I'm up to." And so, on gallops Blitzen as darkness falls and the stars come out. Now Rupert sees that all the countryside below is covered in snow and he has a feeling that they are nearly there.

Then quite suddenly the nice safe feeling is gone! Blitzen is galloping faster and faster as if drawn by something it can hear which Rupert can't. "S-steady, Blitzen!" Rupert pleads. "Oh, do slow down!" But the reindeer scarcely seems to hear him. And now it is beginning to head for the snow-covered ground. Then in the moonlight Rupert sees what Blitzen seems to be heading for – a cluster of moving shadows on the snow. They're . . . yes . . . yes, they're reindeer!

23

RUPERT FINDS THE REINDEER

Then suddenly they're on the ground
With Santa's reindeer standing round.

"What do you want here, little bear?"
A girl on skis is standing there.

"Those reindeer don't belong to you.
They're Santa's and they're overdue."

She stares at Rupert with dismay
Then turns about and speeds away.

Rupert braces himself for an awful bump when they land but the landing is so smooth that for a moment he hardly realises that they are down. What's more, they are right in the middle of the cluster of reindeer he saw from the air, and from the way they look at Blitzen and Blitzen looks at them he knows they are Santa's. Before he can gather his breath to speak Rupert hears the swish of something skimming over the snow and turns to face a young girl on skis. She is carrying a bell.

The girl doesn't look very friendly and when she speaks she doesn't sound it either: "What do you want here, small bear, among my reindeer?" "*Your* reindeer?" Rupert gasps. "They're Santa's and I've been sent to fetch them home where they should have been ages ago." The girl stares at him but says nothing. Then in a twinkling she spins round And swoops away across the moonlit snow. "What a very odd girl," thinks Rupert. "Saying Santa's reindeer were hers."

RUPERT TAKES A TUMBLE

"You've upset Santa, you reindeer!"
Cries Rupert. "Let's get out of here!"

Just when it seems they might obey,
That bell sounds and they race away.

A branch sweeps Rupert to the ground.
His mount pursues the tinkling sound.

He sits up with a groan and sees
It disappearing through the trees.

With the girl gone, Rupert turns to the reindeer. "You should be jolly well ashamed of yourselves!" he begins. "Poor Santa is terribly worried. Without you how could he get people's Christmas presents to them?" The reindeer look ashamed. "Right, we are going home now!" Rupert says sternly. But it is not to be as easy as that. Suddenly, from trees on a nearby ridge comes the tinkling of a bell such as Rupert has never heard. The reindeer prick their ears then bolt towards the sound.

Blitzen hesitates for only an instant before racing after the others with Rupert clinging to its neck. "Stop! Whoa! Come back, you lot!" he cries. But the reindeer cannot resist the tinkling of that strange bell. Into the forest they plunge with the tinkling growing louder. Then in the moment Rupert sees the girl swinging the bell, a low branch sweeps him from the saddle. The thick snow saves him from being hurt. But he sits up in time to see the last reindeer disappear into the night.

RUPERT GETS A SURPRISE

He trails his mount. Its tracks are clear.
Then snow falls and they disappear.

The night's too dark, the snow too deep.
Exhausted, Rupert falls asleep.

He wakes to feel a cosy glow.
A robe protects him from the snow.

"Although the 'deer you've come to seize
I could not leave you here to freeze."

This is awful! Just when he thought he was doing so well. Now here he is without even the reindeer he came on, and lost in a freezing forest into the bargain. There's only one thing for it – he must follow the reindeer tracks. So off he sets, plodding gamely through the trees . . . then it begins to snow! In seconds the tracks vanish under the new snow. Lost, cold and oh, so terribly tired, Rupert does what you should never do at times like these. He lies down in the snow to sleep . . .

Rupert stirs. Slowly he begins to waken. For a moment he can't think where he is. Oh, yes! Lost in the snowy forest. The last thing he can remember is the falling snow and the cold. But what's this? he feels almost cosy. His eyes snap open. He is lying near a crackling fire. A thick robe has been laid over him. And standing by the fire is the girl. She is heating something in a can. And, oh, doesn't it smell good! Santa's reindeer are standing nearby. The girl gives a little smile.

RUPERT HEARS RIKA'S STORY

"I'm Rika and I love reindeer.
But girls may not have such things here."

"She's helped me so I'll help her too.
I think I know what I can do."

To Santa she agrees to go,
But first she'll let her parents know.

Her father says he thinks she's wise
To go off and apologise.

"Who are you? Why did you come back?" Rupert asks, sipping soup from the can the girl hands him. She sighs: "My name is Rika. I couldn't leave you to freeze. So I came back and brought your reindeer." But why did she take them to start with, Rupert wants to know. "I belong to the Lapp people," Rika says. "We love reindeer. They are our wealth. But girls may not herd them, and I so want to, and when I saw those that didn't seem to belong to anyone, well . . ." And just then Rupert has an idea.

"I think I know how I can help her," he tells himself. Aloud he says. "I think it's important that you come back with me and tell Santa you're sorry you kept his reindeer." Rika looks as if she doesn't much fancy the idea but she says, "Yes, I suppose you're right. I shall have to ask my father." And so some time later Rupert is being led into the Lapp family's camp. When Rika's parents hear her own up to what she has done and what Rupert suggests, they agree that she can go.

RUPERT TELLS SANTA HIS IDEA

With Rupert leading, off they fly
To Santa's through the wintry sky.

Santa himself is waiting when
The reindeer get back home again.

Rika tells him she's sorry and
Santa smiles, "There, I understand."

"If," Rupert starts, "you'd be so kind – "
Then whispers what he has in mind.

Rika's father finds a reindeer saddle for her and helps her up onto one of Santa's team. "You were naughty," he tells her. "But now you're doing the right thing and I'm sure Santa will understand." So off again into the sky, with Rupert on Blitzen leading the way. The freezing Far North is left behind. The familiar shapes of Nutwood slip by far below as the reindeer speed towards Santa's castle in the clouds. And at last it appears with Santa himself waving a welcome.

Santa is overjoyed to have his reindeer back but he listens gravely while Rika says how sorry she is. Then he smiles, pats her head and says, "There, I quite understand and you're forgiven." Then he turns to Rupert who is tugging his sleeve: "And what can I do for you?" "May I have a word alone with you?" Rupert asks. "It will have to be quick. I'm very busy," Santa says. So while Rika gazes at all the bustle as presents are loaded, Rupert tells Santa his idea.

RUPERT SPRINGS A SURPRISE

Then back to Rika Rupert flies
To warn her of a big surprise.

"Please keep this special bell, my dear,
And tend my reindeer every year."

Now in the cowboy's little 'plane
They set off for their homes again.

At Nutwood Rupert leaves his friend.
It's worked out nicely in the end.

When Rupert is done Santa nods and disappears into the castle. Rupert, with a big smile, runs back to Rika. "Oh, Rika!" he bursts out. "You're going to have such a lovely surprise!" And just then Santa emerges. One of his little soldiers is marching before him carrying something on a silk cushion. "A reindeer bell!" gasps Rika. "And a very special one," smiles Santa. He hands the bell to Rika and says, "I hereby appoint you, Rika, the official keeper of my reindeer during their long holidays in the Far North. And be sure you get them back to me in time for Christmas each year." Rika can hardly speak for joy, and she can still hardly believe her luck as she sets off in the cowboy's aircraft for home. The 'plane lands at Nutwood to let Rupert off. When it takes off again Rupert calls after it, "It's been lovely meeting you, Rika. You must come and visit us sometime." And faintly on the wind he hears her call back, "Of course I shall, Rupert!" The End.

RUPERT and

*"I'm off to see if I can find
Some sweet chestnuts – the roasting kind."*

"Where are you off to?" Mr. Bear looks up from his leaf-raking as Rupert appears with a basket. "Mummy wants sweet chestnuts for roasting so I'm going to the woods to get some," Rupert says. "Shan't be long." And off he goes.

Rupert's way to the woods takes him past the home of his magician friend, the Chinese Conjurer. What he sees there makes him stop and stare. A cloud of smoke full of flashing stars!

30

the Worried Elves

But on his way the little bear
Sees something strange that makes him stare.

Star-spangled smoke hangs in the air.
What can his friend be burning there?

Of course Rupert can't resist going in to see what's happening. The smoke, he finds, is coming from the chimney of an outdoor stove into which the Conjurer is feeding something. He does not notice Rupert. Nor at first does his little daughter Tigerlily when she appears with more articles which her father drops into the stove. Then she looks up and sees him. "Rupert!" she cries. "How nice! Daddy, my friend is here!"

Still closer, Rupert can't make out
Just what his Chinese friend's about.

RUPERT SEES OLD MAGIC BURNED

*"I always burn each magic bit
When I've no further use for it."*

*"It is not wise, my Daddy's found
To leave old magic things around."*

*"I've work to do so I can't stay.
I really must be on my way."*

*"The Wise Old Goat. Perhaps he may
Like me be bound the woodland way."*

The Conjurer greets Rupert with a smile. He can see that the little bear is bursting to ask what he is doing. "I destroy old magic things I have no use for now," he explains, holding up one of the articles before dropping it into the stove. "But couldn't you give them away?" Rupert asks him as star-spangled smoke billows. A smile is the only answer Rupert gets. But Tigerlily leads him aside. "In wrong hands magic is very dangerous," she says. "Much safer to burn it."

When he thinks about it, Rupert can see that's the sensible thing to do. So he leaves his two friends to their magic-burning and presses on to the woods. The crisp leaves under his feet remind him that soon the trees will be bare. He sighs: "Sometimes I wish they could be green all year like the things in the Conjurer's strange garden." Just then he spies another clever friend. "It's the Wise Old Goat!" he exclaims. "I haven't seen him for weeks and weeks."

32

RUPERT FINDS THE MIST TREE

"Some sweet chestnuts I hope to find . . .
If any have been left behind!"

How green that tree is over there.
Though other trees are almost bare.

"It does not shed its leaves, this tree,
Until the first mist comes, you see."

"It's kept its leaves – and this is queer,
There's been no autumn mist this year."

Rupert joins the Wise Old Goat who is glad of the company and together they stroll into the woodland. "I'm looking for herbs," says the Goat. "What are you doing?" So Rupert explains that he is after sweet chestnuts. "If," he adds, pointing to a squirrel leaping across their path, "those little rascals leave me any."

A little way on, in the middle of an old ruin, Rupert spots a tree he hasn't seen before. "How very green it looks," he wonders aloud.

"That isn't an ordinary evergreen, is it?" he asks the Wise Old Goat.

"No," his friend says. "It is very rare – a Mist Tree. It's the only one in this part of the world. It will shed its leaves, though." "But they have not even begun to fall," Rupert points out.

The Goat smiles. "That is the reason for its name. Its leaves won't fall until the first mist of autumn." And Rupert thinks, "That's odd. There hasn't been a sign of mist this autumn."

RUPERT SURPRISES TWO ELVES

"No, let those leaves alone, I say,
Or else the tree will die away!

Now Rupert searches all around
But not a chestnut's to be found.

A creaking noise! A heavy stone
Seems to be rising on its own!

They're startled, those two Autumn Elves
To find that they're not by themselves.

As he gazes at the Mist Tree Rupert decides to pick some leaves to show his teacher. But as he reaches for them the Wise Old Goat cries, "No, you must not!" Then he explains, "This is not like other trees. If you pick its leaves now it will wither and die. You must wait until they fall by themselves. Do you know, in bygone days the Mist Tree was thought to have the wonderful power of making the air fresh and sweet." So, of course Rupert heeds his friend's warning and the

Wise Old Goat leaves him to his chestnut search.

But there isn't a chestnut to be found. Those squirrels, it seems, have already been here. Then just when Rupert is about to move on he hears a creaking and spins round to see a rock rising as if pushed up by something underground. And his eyes pop as from below the rock emerge two tiny creatures. For a moment they don't notice Rupert. Then they turn and see him. "Eeek!" they squeal. "It's all right, it's only me," says Rupert.

RUPERT LEARNS WHY NO MIST

"Could you two Autumn Elves make clear
Why there has been no mist this year."

"Our mist pots are kept locked and we
Must wait 'til someone brings a key."

"We cannot leave our posts and so
Perhaps to fetch the key you'd go."

Before a good excuse he's found
The Elves have led him underground.

Of course, Rupert has recognised the new-comers. They are Autumn Elves. They live underground and Rupert has met them on several of his adventures. "You're just the people I want to see," he says. "Being in charge of things like mist and heavy dew, can you tell me why there has been no mist this autumn?" For answer the Elves lead him to three small stone pots, each with a padlock. "We can't release the mist until the inspector comes to open these chimneys," says one.

"Why hasn't the inspector come?" Rupert asks. "He's too busy," an Elf replies. "The smoke-gathering machinery at our headquarters is out of order and he's trying to find out what's wrong. We daren't leave our Nutwood post to collect the key for the chimneys from him. But there's nothing to stop you!" And before Rupert can think of an excuse he is being led back to where he met the Elves and ushered down the steps below that rock he saw rising just a short while back.

RUPERT RIDES THE TRAVEL POLE

*He knows the Elves' rail cars of old
But can't use them this time, he's told.*

*"This is the way that you must go.
You'll find it really fast, you know."*

*"You're travelling at quite a height,
So, do remember, hold on tight!"*

*"If you should want the pole to slow
There is a brake – now off you GO!"*

"Are you sure I'm the one to help you," Rupert protests feebly as he is hustled along a passage. "Maybe the inspector won't give me the key." "Of course, he will," the Elves chorus. They pass a little rail-car Rupert recognises. "I've ridden on one of those to your headquarters before," he says. "That's Route One," replies an Elf. "You don't go that way. It's Route Two for you." And on they go, stopping only when they reach a sort of overhead track.

"You'll have to use our travelling pole," one of the Elves tells Rupert as they lead the way on to a platform. "Stand on that footrest at the foot of the pole," Rupert is instructed. "And hold very tight to the pole itself. There's a brake you can use if you get up too much speed."

Well, Rupert does as he's told, and as soon as he is in position the Elves chorus, "Ready, steady . . . GO!" And they give one mighty push which sends Rupert hurtling away.

RUPERT MEETS THE INSPECTOR

Before too long he finds the run
Is really quite surprising fun.

At last the journey ends and he
Sees this is where he gets the key.

He peeks inside and sees an Elf
Who's busy working by himself.

"This smoke," he mutters, "baffles me.
What's wrong with it's a mystery."

Rupert has travelled on all sorts of machines on his adventures. But this travelling-pole is as breath-taking as any. He grasps the pole as hard as he can while it whisks him faster and faster through the underground passages. Then he recalls that one of the Elves mentioned a brake. Yes, there it is. A handle on the pole. He pulls it and at once the speed slackens and he begins to enjoy his trip. It ends outside a door marked "District Inspector".

Rupert climbs down from the travelling-pole and knocks on the door. Nothing. He knocks again and still gets no answer. So he pushes the door and peeps inside. At the far end of a room an Autumn Elf is working at a bench. He is so caught up in what he is doing that he is quite unaware that Rupert is there. "He must be the inspector," Rupert decides and tiptoes forward, not sure if he should disturb him. The Elf is studying a test-tube full of smoke and shaking his head.

RUPERT SEES MAGIC SMOKE

He says, when he sees Rupert there,
"Ah, you can help here, little bear!"

"Now take this tube and hold it tight
While I switch on this special light."

"I know from using those light rays,
There's magic in that smoke," he says.

"I saw my friend in Nutwood stoke
His stove with stuff that made that smoke."

"Ahem!" Rupert coughs politely. "Excuse me." The Elf spins round. "Well, what do you want?" he demands, and without waiting for an answer goes on impatiently, "Well, whoever you are, there is no need to stand around being useless. Hold this! He thrusts the test-tube into Rupert's hands and hustles him in front of some sort of machine. "Now stand still," he orders. But that isn't easy for when he switches on the machine and rays from it strike the test-tube, Rupert tingles and shakes all over.

"It won't harm you," the Elf assures him, but Rupert is still glad when the machine is switched off. The Elf offers him a seat and says, "You felt tingly because that smoke has magic in it. Now I know why our smoke-gathering machinery won't work. Look at this." He leads Rupert to a tank full of smoke. "I've collected all that. It comes from Nutwood way." Rupert stares. "It's exactly the same as the smoke the Conjurer was making!" he exclaims.

RUPERT IS TAKEN OFF AGAIN

"The smoke machine we Elves use here
Can't handle magic smoke, I fear."

"Let's take our news and bring some joy
To our poor worried Basement Boy."

"You only came to get a key?
Well, here it is. Now come with me!"

"Our smoke-collecting plant is where
We're going on that thing, young bear."

As Rupert explains what he means about the smoke being like the stuff from the Conjurer's stove, the Elf inspector's face lights up. "That's it!" he cries. "The magic must still have been in the smoke when it reached our headquarters. Of course, our machinery went wrong. It's only meant to cope with ordinary smoke, not magic stuff!" Then he grabs Rupert by the hand. "Come on!" he chuckles. "We're going to see the Basement Boy. He's been terribly worried about all this."

"But I only came for a key," protests Rupert as the inspector pulls him towards another door. "The Autumn Elves in Nutwood need it to open their mist pots." "No trouble!" cries the Elf and he unhooks a key which he gives to Rupert. "Now this way!" He flings open the door revealing a trolley of some kind on a track. "This is Route Three," he announces. 'It will take us to where we are going – to the smoke-collecting machinery at our head-quarters. Now let's hurry!"

RUPERT DRIVES A TROLLEY

*"This trolley doesn't drive itself.
We have to pump it," says the Elf.*

*Yet Rupert finds there's not much need
To pump hard when they pick up speed.*

*Now thicker clouds of mist appear.
The little Elf cries, "Stop! We're here!"*

*The Elves' headquarters buildings rise
Above the mist which round them lies.*

As Rupert climbs aboard the trolley the Elf says, "Now, this isn't like Routes One and Two. On Route Three we have to work!" He lays down the test-tube of smoke carefully then takes his place opposite Rupert. "These handles," he explains, "are like a see-saw and we have to push them up and down to make the thing go." And so they set to work – and jolly hard work it is at first. But soon the little trolley is rattling along the narrow track faster and faster.

As the trolley gathers speed Rupert finds it easier to pump the handle up and down. "I'm quite enjoying this!" he laughs. "Is there much further to go?" "No, we're nearly there, it's beginning to get misty," the Elf says. On they go with the mist getting thicker all the time until they reach the end of the line. Rupert can tell they are out of the tunnel. But where? "Our headquarters!" the Elf tells him. "Look, you can see the buildings above the mist. Now just a short walk."

RUPERT MEETS THE BRAINY ELF

*The Elves are bored because they can't
Now work their smoke-collecting plant.*

*The Elf inspector tells them, though,
Their plant can soon be made to go.*

*As down they go the Elf explains,
"The Basement Boy's our one with brains."*

*They find him pacing to and fro
And muttering, "Why won't it go?"*

Rupert gazes about him as he follows his guide to the Autumn Elves' headquarters. The elf workers are sitting about doing nothing and looking bored. "This is where the smoke is gathered," says the inspector. "It's our job to keep the air clean. That's why we were worried when things went wrong." He stops beside a group of workers to tell them the good news. "This little bear has solved the mystery," he announces. "It won't be long before you're busy again." They all cheer.

The inspector leads on to a lift. "Now we go to see the Basement Boy," he says. "He's really brainy . . ." "Like the Backroom Boy the Imps of Spring have," chimes in Rupert. "Right!" says the inspector. "But we don't have a back room so we had to put him in the basement."

At last the lift stops and the pair get out. They are in a sort of workshop and striding up and down it is a worried-looking Elf wearing glasses. "What can have gone wrong?" he keeps muttering.

RUPERT SEES THE BRAIN BOX

"Your problem's answered here inside
This tube of smoke!" cries Rupert's guide.

Then Rupert's called on to explain
About the magic smoke again.

The Basement Boy cries "Just watch me.
I'm going to find the remedy."

"The Brain Box here, without a doubt,
Will tell us how to sort it out."

"You can stop worrying! We've got the answer!" Holding out the test-tube the inspector breaks in on the Basement Boy's muttering. "You've what?" squeaks the other. "Is this your idea of a joke?" "No, it's true!" insists the inspector. "This little bear here will tell you what went wrong." Rupert is ushered forward to explain about the smoke from the Conjurer's magic-burning and how the inspector proved that it still had magic in it when it reached the Elves' machinery.

"Of course! Magic smoke!" cries the Basement Boy. "Why didn't I think of that? Now all we need is the remedy. And my Brain Box will come up with that." He crosses to a wall panel and presses a number of buttons. "I've asked it the question," he says. "Let's see what its answer is."

Rupert doesn't understand. "A machine answer a question?" he gasps. "How? It can't think surely!" "Just you wait!" chuckles the Basement Boy. "My Brain Box never fails!"

RUPERT LEARNS THE REMEDY

The Brain Box whirls and clicks and hums.
Then from a slot a card there comes.

To read the code upon the card,
The Basement Boy says, isn't hard.

"Ah, yes," he murmurs, "Let me see.
We need leaves from the rare Mist Tree."

They gasp when they hear Rupert say
He's seen just such a tree today.

A lot of whirring and clicking goes on while Rupert waits and wonders. He is about to ask how long the Brain Box will take to find the answer when suddenly a card shoots from a slot and lands beside him. He picks it up and studies it. He frowns. "Is this the answer?" he asks. "It is nothing but dots and dashes. It isn't a message at all." "Oh, but it is!" insists the Basement Boy. "It's all a matter of being able to understand it. You can't. I can."

The Basement Boy takes the card from Rupert and examines it. "H'mm" he repeats several times. And, "Good!" Finally he turns to the others and says, "The answer is to find leaves of the Mist Tree and burn them with the magic things that have caused all the trouble. That will stop the smoke from being troublesome." He pauses. "Not easy, though," he muses. "Mist Trees are very rare."

"But there's one in our woods at home!" Rupert cries. "I saw it only this morning!"

RUPERT RETURNS TO NUTWOOD

"Then go and get those leaves!" they cry.
"Don't hang about. You've got to fly!"

"Into the rail-car. Off with you!
We're sure that you know what to do."

And now that he is Nutwood bound,
He races full tilt underground.

An Elf is waiting for him when
He reaches Nutwood once again.

The Autumn Elves listen eagerly as Rupert tells of coming across the Mist Tree with the Wise Old Goat and what his friend told him about it. "He said its leaves won't fall until the first mist of autumn."

"That's the tree right enough!" the Basement Boy cries. "Our troubles are over. Now back you go to Nutwood. You know what to do!" Rupert is bundled through a doorway marked "Route 1" and told, "It's the quickest way back. Good luck!"

Rupert has driven one of the little rail cars before and remembers what to do. Slowly he moves the control rod, letting the car gather speed gradually. He switches on the powerful lights so that he can see the bends coming up and slow down for them. And there are plenty of twists and turns on Route One. As he approaches the end of the line one of the Nutwood Autumn Elves is waiting for him. "You've been quite a while," he greets the little bear. "I hope you've got that key."

RUPERT RELEASES THE MIST

He tells his tale, says, "Here's the key.
Now, hurry, make some mist for me."

"Since, Rupert, you the key have brought,
Then you shall open our first pot."

A soft white haze comes seeping out.
"At last, our mist!" the two Elves shout.

As Rupert leaves he thinks, "That's good!
The mist is drifting to the wood."

"I've not only got the key from the inspector," Rupert says proudly. "I also found out what was causing the trouble at your headquarters." And he tells them about the Conjurer's magic smoke and how the Elves' machinery could not cope with it. "But everything will be all right if I give the Conjurer some Mist Tree leaves to burn with his magic things. But I can't pick them until there is a mist or the tree will wither." "Then let's get busy," chorus the Elves and scamper up to their smoke pots on the surface. "You," one of them tells Rupert, "must have the honour of opening the first of them." So Rupert undoes the padlock, lifts the lid and sees a white cloud pour from the pot. To his delight it drifts towards the wood where the Mist Tree is.

Rupert picks up the basket he left there earlier and says, "I must get to the Mist Tree right away." And off he hurries, leaving the happy Elves jigging around the opened mist pot.

RUPERT COLLECTS THE LEAVES

He tells himself, "I must be quick.
This mist is getting really thick."

Then what he sees he scarce believes.
The Mist Tree's shedding all its leaves!

Today's green leaves, now they are down,
Like autumn leaves are dry and brown.

A squirrel squeaks, "Please come back, do.
We've kept a share of nuts for you."

The mist is spreading quickly and by the time Rupert reaches the woods the trees are just dim shapes. As he hurries along he thinks, "It's so thick now I could easily get lost. That would be awful, getting lost in the mist I helped to make." Then suddenly, just visible through the white haze he catches sight of the Mist Tree. Its leaves are falling in a gentle shower and the branches are bare by the time Rupert reaches it. He is sorry the Wise Old Goat couldn't see this.

Rupert marvels as he kneels to gather up the leaves of the Mist Tree. "Such a little time ago they were all fresh and green. Now they're brown and dry. It must have happened as soon as the mist touched them."

Rupert fills his basket with leaves and starts back through the misty woods. Suddenly from a tree a squirrel calls to him. "I heard you say you're after sweet chestnuts," it squeaks. "We've got lots. Come back later for a share of them."

RUPERT SEES THE MAGIC VANISH

"What brings you back here, little bear?
And what is in your basket there?"

And then with real dismay he learns
What happens when his magic burns.

"The leaves, you say, will make all well!
Then in they go to break the spell!"

See! All at once the smoke is clear.
The stars and flashes disappear.

Rupert thanks the kindly squirrel and hurries on to the Conjurer's house. He finds the magician in his garden still burning his old magic things. "Back again?" he says inquiringly when the little bear appears. So Rupert explains about the trouble the magic-burning has caused to the Autumn Elves. "And that's why I'm here again," he says. "I've brought these leaves from the Mist Tree. If you burn them along with your old magic things they'll take the magic out of the smoke."

The Conjurer who is a very considerate man is dismayed about having caused so much trouble. "Must put this right at once," he says. "I did not think that my old magic could do any harm when it had been burnt." And at once he starts putting handfuls of Mist Tree leaves into the stove. Just then Tigerlily appears. She starts to ask what is going on then she catches sight of the smoke from the stove. "Look, no stars in it now!" she cries. "Yes, the magic has gone!" Rupert laughs.

RUPERT'S DADDY IS AMAZED

They take deep breaths. How sweet the air
Is now there is no magic there.

"A squirrel's kept some nuts for me,
But first I'm going home for tea."

Says Mr. Bear, "You should have seen
How black that smoke was. Now it's clean!"

Then Rupert laughs, "Wait 'til you hear
How my friends get the air so clear!"

As the three friends watch the smoke rise, the Conjurer takes a deep breath. "The air – it is so fresh and sweet," he marvels. And Rupert remembers what the Wise Old Goat told him. "Long ago," he tells the others, "people believed that the Mist Tree kept the air fresh. It seems to be true."

Tigerlily walks Rupert to the gate and he tells her of his adventures with the Autumn Elves. "And now I'm off home," he finishes. "Then I'm going to get some chestnuts I've been promised."

Mr. Bear is still in the garden when Rupert gets home. "You know, I made a bonfire," he tells the little bear, "and at first the smoke hung about in an awful cloud. Now, it's going away nicely." "That just shows the Autumn Elves' machinery is working again," Rupert says. Then he sees that Mr. Bear doesn't understand and he laughs: "It's a long story, Daddy. And I must say I'm more than just a bit hungry. I'll tell you and Mummy about it over tea." The End.

Rupert's Paper Banger

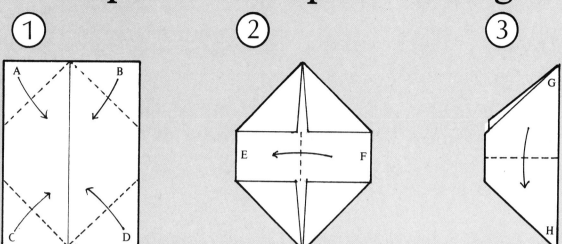

Take a thin, strong piece of paper about the size of this page. Start by folding it in half lengthwise to give you a middle line (1). Fold the points A,B,C, and D to that middle line (2).
Now fold side F to side E to get (3).

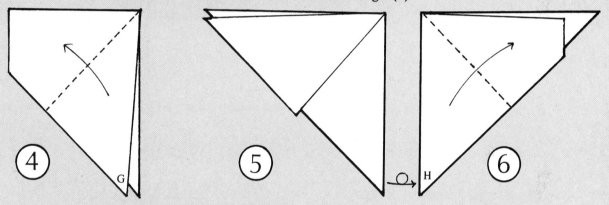

Fold point G to point H which leaves you with (4). Fold point G up as shown by the arrow to give you (5). Now turn the model over (6) and fold up point H as indicated by the arrow.
This leaves you with the completed model (7).

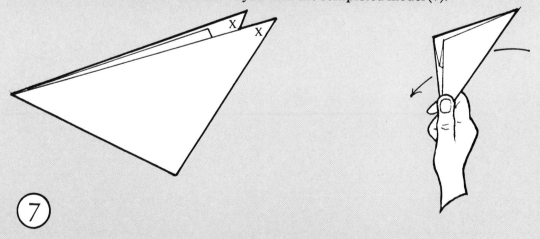

Hold the model firmly between forefinger and thumb at the points marked X. Raise it above your head and bring it down sharply…BANG!

RUPERT and

The breeze is brisk, the sun is bright.
It's just the day to fly a kite.

It is a bright, breezy morning, just the sort of day for kite-flying, and Rupert has gone up to Pong-Ping's house to try out his new one. Being Chinese, Pong-Ping is good with kites and he soon shows Rupert how to make this one swoop and soar. His pet dragon loves this and dashes about pretending to chase the kite. Then suddenly Pong-Ping stops laughing. "Look, Constable Growler's coming this way," he says. "And he looks grim."

he Dragon Mystery

*Then Pong-Ping stops and says, "I fear
The village policeman's coming here."*

*It's P.C. Growler, looking grim.
Still, Pong-Ping is polite to him.*

Puffing a bit after his ride from Nutwood, the
village policeman dismounts. "Good morning,"
Pong-Ping greets him politely. "Can I help you?"
But there is no smile in return from Growler. "I've
come on a serious matter," he announces, taking
out his notebook. "It's about your pet dragon there.
I've had complaints he's been eating vegetables in
people's gardens and taking food from a stall
outside a shop. What have you to say, eh?"

*"Food's been stolen. Though he's tame,
Folks say your dragon pet's to blame.*

John Harrold

51

RUPERT'S FRIEND IS CAUTIONED

"No, no! It spends all day at home.
It never is allowed to roam!"

"Now pay good heed to what I say,
More stealing and it's locked away!"

The policeman's gone, but so's the pet,
A fact which makes poor Pong-Ping fret.

They find it and they guess it fled
Because of what the policeman said.

Well, Rupert and Pong-Ping can't believe their ears. The little dragon raiding gardens and taking food from shops? "Impossible!" bursts out Pong-Ping indignantly. "My pet is at home almost all the time and I only ever take it out on its fine gold chain!" But Growler is not at all impressed. "Fact remains," he says, "people have actually seen the dragon up to its mischief and yours is the only dragon I know of around here. Any more of it and I'll have to lock it up."

With that warning, Constable Growler gets on his bike and pedals away.

"How can anyone believe that you do such things?" Pong-Ping demands, turning to his pet. But it has gone. "Maybe it slipped indoors while Constable Growler was talking," Rupert suggests. And sure enough, inside the house the pals find the dragon hiding behind a screen looking frightened. "It must have heard what that policeman said about being locked up," whispers Pong-Ping.

RUPERT SEES SOMETHING ODD

The policeman's charges it denies.
And Pong-Ping knows it never lies.

Rupert also thinks that's true,
Though people saw a dragon, too.

Next day at breakfast, Mr. Bear
Cries "What's that in the garden there?"

Then through the window Rupert peeks.
A dragon's there among the leeks!

Oh, so gently – because he is very fond of the little creature – Pong-Ping coaxes the dragon from behind the screen. At once it begins to chatter and squeak at Pong-Ping while Rupert looks on not understanding. When it stops Pong-Ping explains: "It says it is absolutely amazed at what that policeman said. It has done none of the things he said people had complained about. And I believe it!" "So do I," says Rupert loyally. "But then what was the dragon so many people have seen?"

At breakfast next day Rupert is starting to tell his parents about the mystery of the dragon when Mr. Bear leaps to his feet and goes to the window. "Something's got into our vegetable patch," he says. Then he rushes out. "What is it?" Rupert calls after him. "I couldn't quite see," Mr. Bear calls back. So Rupert climbs onto his chair and peers out of the window. And, yes, something is moving in the vegetable patch, among the leeks, in fact – something with a dragon's tail!

RUPERT TELLS PONG-PING

"I couldn't find the thing, I fear.
Did you see what it was my dear?"

"I saw it with my own two eyes,
A little dragon!" Rupert cries.

To Pong-Ping's house he runs. He's keen
To tell his pal what he has seen.

But Pong-Ping cries, "To think that you,
A pal, would blame my dragon, too!"

Rupert is still standing on his chair staring out of the window when Mr. Bear comes back. "I was just too late," he pants. "Whatever it was had gone by the time I got outside. Could either of you see anything?" Mrs. Bear shakes her head. Rupert climbs down from the chair. "I'm sure I saw something," he begins slowly. "Well – what was it?" asks Mr. Bear. "I – I think it was a dragon!" Rupert says. As his parents gasp in astonishment, Rupert wonders what Pong-Ping's going to say.

So, straight after breakfast Rupert hurries off to find Pong-Ping and tell him what he has seen. As he runs towards his friend's big Chinese house he keeps seeing again in his mind that creature among his Daddy's vegetables.

When he bursts into the house announcing, "I saw a dragon in our vegetable patch this morning!" Pong-Ping snatches up his pet and cries, "Not you as well! My pet's been with me all morning so don't try to tell me it was in your garden!"

RUPERT'S PAL MISUNDERSTANDS

*"Now, Pong-Ping, please don't get upset!
I didn't say it was your pet."*

*"It was not yours, I am quite clear.
So yours has nothing now to fear."*

*"We must tell Growler what you say.
Let's find him now, without delay!"*

*The pals have hardly started when
They see that Growler's back again.*

Pong-Ping plants himself in a chair with his dragon on his knee and glares at Rupert. "To think a close friend like you would go around saying my dragon was stealing from his garden! You were here when it told me it had done nothing wrong . . ." Rupert holds up his hand. "I said I saw a dragon," he smiles. "Not that I saw *your* dragon." "I – I don't understand," stammers Pong-Ping. "Nor do I," agrees Rupert. "But I didn't think it looked like your dragon. Now I'm sure."

Pong-Ping jumps up. "Another dragon altogether!" he cries. "Here in Nutwood! But how . . . ? Are you quite sure, Rupert?" "Quite, quite sure!" Rupert laughs, happy that his friend is no longer cross. "And that's why Constable Growler looked as if he didn't believe me when I said it couldn't have been my pet," reasons Pong-Ping. "A dragon was seen, all right. But not mine! Let's go and tell him!" But they don't have to, for Growler is on his way to see them.

RUPERT TELLS THE POLICEMAN

Pong-Ping's high humour fades away
When P.C. Growler has his say.

"One more complaint. This time it's bad.
For this one comes from Rupert's Dad!"

He tells Pong-Ping that Mr. Bear
Says Rupert saw his dragon there.

"Not Pong-Ping's dragon!" Rupert cries.
And Growler knows he never lies.

This time Pong-Ping is glad to see the village policeman and runs to meet him. "About my dragon," he begins. But Growler breaks in, "Yes, about your dragon!" Rupert and Pong-Ping don't understand and wait for the policeman to continue. Looking very stern Growler says, "Remember what I said before? Any more trouble from your dragon and it would have to be locked up. Well, there has been another complaint about it taking vegetables . . . and it came from your Daddy, Rupert Bear!"

Rupert and Pong-Ping are quite speechless. A complaint from Rupert's Daddy! Pong-Ping turns to Rupert in dismay but the little bear is just as puzzled as he is. "So locked up it will have to be," Growler adds. "Sorry about this. But Mr. Bear says it was Rupert who actually saw it." At that Rupert's face lights up. "Oh, but that certainly was not Pong-Ping's dragon!" he cries. "It was a different dragon altogether. I didn't *think* it was then, and I'm sure now."

RUPERT HELPS TO SEARCH

*"Well, that is that," says Pong-Ping, "yet
I feel he still suspects my pet."*

*"Let's find the other one!" they say,
But find Pong-Ping's has run away.*

*They find no trace of it although
They search Pong-Ping's house high and low.*

*"We know that other one's to blame.
Now other folk may say the same."*

Growler knows Rupert doesn't tell lies so he says, "Ah! H'm!" and remounts his bike. But before he goes he turns and asks, "The 'other' dragon, how was it different?" "Darker," Rupert says. "Not the same shape as Pong-Ping's." Growler repeats, "H'm!" and leaves. After a moment Pong-Ping says, "He still half-suspects my pet. I vote we find the other one just to show him." "Right," Rupert agrees. "Maybe your pet has some ideas." But there is no sign of it in the garden now.

"It must have run off to hide when it heard the policeman talking about locking it up," Pong-Ping says. But though the pals search the house high and low they can't find it. "Try the garden then," Rupert suggests. "And while you are doing that I'll go back to Nutwood and talk to all the people who say they saw this mysterious dragon. If they saw it as clearly as I did it shouldn't be difficult to get them to agree that it was not your pet." "Good idea!" says Pong-Ping.

RUPERT ASKS QUESTIONS

*"I can't be sure. 'Twas just a peek
I got when that thing stole a leek."*

*He keeps on coming back to leeks.
Is this the vital clue he seeks?*

*Yes, in among the leeks is where
The thing was seen by Mr. Bear.*

*Then at the gate Pong-Ping appears.
The poor thing's very close to tears.*

So Rupert hurries back to Nutwood where first he calls on the greengrocer. "Yes," says the man, "The dragon snatched a leek from this very box and ran off before I could get it." "But was it Pong-Ping's dragon?" Rupert asks. The man hesitates then says, "I can't be sure. But how many dragons are there around here?" Rupert gets the same sort of answers from a gardener. What dragon could it have been but Pong-Ping's at his leeks? Leeks? Leeks! An idea begins to form in Rupert's mind.

As he scurries round to his own cottage Rupert thinks, "We always seem to come back to leeks. Now, leeks and dragons? Dragons and leeks?" The idea is growing. He finds Mr. Bear in the garden. "Daddy, where exactly did you see the dragon?" he asks. "There," Mr. Bear points to the leeks. "Yes, that's where I thought I remembered seeing it, too," Rupert says. But before he can say any more Pong-Ping appears at the garden gate. He is the picture of dismay. Something must be badly wrong.

RUPERT TRIES OUT HIS IDEA

"My dragon's slipped his chain and run
Away to find the other one."

"Those leeks gave me a clue, you see,
To what that other one may be!"

Dragons, winged, with curly tails,
And leeks? Of course they come from Wales!

"And somehow such a dragon's found
Its way to Nutwood, I'll be bound!"

"I found this by my side gate!" cries Pong-Ping. He holds up his dragon's collar. "It really has run away this time. I'm sure it has gone off to find the other dragon." "What other dragon?" Mr. Bear wants to know. So Rupert explains: "I was just going to tell you that the dragon I saw here was not Pong-Ping's and that I have an idea about it. It has all to do with leeks." "Leeks!" Mr. Bear is more puzzled than ever. So is Pong-Ping. What have leeks to do with it, they ask.

So Rupert leads the way indoors where he gets down one of his books. As he turns the pages he speaks: "I noticed that this mysterious dragon always took leeks. Then I remembered the leek is the emblem of Wales and . . ." Just then he finds the page he wants and there under "Wales" is the picture of a leek and . . . "A Welsh dragon!" Pong-Ping shouts. "Right!" laughs Rupert. "Somehow a Welsh dragon has found its way to Nutwood. But how? That's what we must find out."

RUPERT ALARMS GREGORY

"Ah, Wales! Let's see," says Mrs. Bear.
"The Guineapigs have just been there."

When "dragon's" mentioned and then "Wales",
Poor Gregory just gasps and quails.

"You do know something, I can see,
About this dragon mystery!"

The young one grabs the chance to flee
When Mummy calls him in for tea.

Mrs. Bear who has been listening to this looks up from her knitting. "Wales," she says. "Now let me see . . . someone we know went to Wales for their holidays . . . yes, Mr. and Mrs. Guineapig took Gregory there. They can't have been back long. Perhaps they may have some ideas."

The pals are not hopeful but they decide to call on Gregory anyway, just in case. They find him at his garden gate. "Did you learn anything in Wales about dragons?" Rupert asks.

Rupert's sudden question quite clearly upsets Gregory. He can't hide his dismay. "I say, you do know something about all this dragon mystery!" cries Pong-Ping fiercely. "Come on, own up!" But at that moment Gregory's Mummy calls him and he scuttles gratefully indoors without a word to the chums. "He certainly does know something!" Pong-Ping exclaims as Gregory disappears. "Somehow we have to find out what." Rupert nods. "For your dragon's sake we must," he says.

RUPERT INVESTIGATES

It's getting rather late and so
The two pals part and homeward go.

"Now, why should Gregory be out
So late and searching all about?"

But then the little bear he sees,
Looks guilty and indoors he flees.

What's that? A sort of rustling sound.
He pushes in and looks around.

Rupert walks part of the way home with Pong-Ping while they discuss Gregory and the dismay he showed when they asked him about Wales and dragons. They agree that since plainly Gregory feels guilty about whatever it is, he is not likely to confess to them. Then as it is late, Rupert turns back. He is passing Gregory's home when something catches his eye. He goes closer and looks over the hedge. Gregory in his dressing-gown is roaming about in the dusk.

Unaware that Rupert is watching him, Gregory goes round his garden, peering behind trees, into flower-beds and under bushes. It is clear that his Mummy doesn't know he is out of doors. Suddenly he looks up, sees Rupert and scampers indoors. Now, what was he up to, Rupert wonders. He is about to turn away for home when something stops him. A rustling in the bushes. Could this be what Gregory was looking for? Agog with excitement, Rupert pushes open the gate and goes in.

RUPERT HATCHES A PLAN

There's something here he should explore.
Yes, look! A shape he's seen before!

"He knows the dragon's there, no doubt,
And that is why he's peeping out."

Next morning Rupert rushes round
To tell Pong-Ping what he has found.

At Gregory's they plan to wait
In hiding when it's getting late.

Rupert shuts the gate quietly behind him and stands perfectly still, holding his breath and listening hard. Yes, there it is again. The same rustling among the bushes. He tiptoes towards the sound and he is just in time to make out in the dusk the tail of a small dragon disappearing into the dense shrubs. This time he is in no doubt. That was most certainly not Pong-Ping's dragon! As he makes his way out of the garden he sees Gregory peeping out from behind his curtains.

Rupert can hardly wait to tell Pong-Ping what he has seen in Gregory's garden and right after breakfast next day he hurries to his friend's house. It is a very worried Pong-Ping who comes to the door. "I've searched everywhere," he says. "But still I can't find a trace of my dragon. He really must have gone off after that other one." Then Rupert tells him what he has seen and at once Pong-Ping perks up. "Find that dragon and we find mine," he says. "Here's what we'll do!"

RUPERT SPRINGS A TRAP

The night is dark, the trap is set.
The chums have brought along a net.

Gregory pauses near the chums.
He calls. And out the dragon comes.

And now our two spring their surprise.
They leap out. "Got you!" Pong-Ping cries.

The dragon's netted and Pong-Ping
Demands to be told everything.

That evening finds the two pals in Gregory's garden, crouching behind a bush. They can see the side door Gregory used the night before. Rupert has come armed with a stout net on a pole. Then at last the door opens and out tiptoes Gregory in dressing-gown and slippers. He crosses the lawn and stops under a tree. "I say, Mervyn, are you there?" he calls in a low voice. The chums hold their breath and stare as out from the bushes beside Gregory pops . . . a little dragon!

The little dragon looks exactly like the Welsh one in Rupert's book. As Gregory bends to talk to it Pong-Ping leaps from his hiding-place. "Aha!" he cries. "Got you!" Gregory squeaks in alarm and Mervyn dashes across the grass with Rupert close behind. Careful not to hurt the little creature, Rupert brings down his net, trapping it. Meanwhile, Gregory, speechless with dismay, finds himself facing a very indignant Pong-Ping who cries, "Now you're going to tell us everything!"

63

RUPERT HEARS GREGORY'S TALE

Now Mrs. Guineapig comes out,
Exclaiming, "What's this all about?"

"That dragon you have there – I say,
We met that one on holiday!"

"There's quite a lot I want to know
About all this, so in you go!"

"When we got back from holiday
Mervyn appeared. He'd stowed away."

Mervyn, the Welsh dragon is still struggling under Rupert's net. "Now, please stop that," says Rupert gently. "No one is going to harm you." And gradually the little creature gives up trying to break out of the net and even smiles at Rupert.

Pong-Ping still hasn't got anything at all out of Gregory when Mrs. Guineapig appears, demanding to know what on earth's going on. Then she points. "That's the little dragon we met in Wales!" she gasps. "What is it doing here?" When she gets no answer she says, "Right, we shall all go indoors and talk about this." Since Mervyn shows no sign of wanting to escape Rupert frees it from the net and it happily follows the others.

"Now what's this about, Gregory?" Mr. Guineapig demands. "It was Mervyn," Gregory begins. "He kept saying he wanted to see the world when we were on holiday. Somehow he managed to hide in my luggage when we were leaving and I didn't find him until we were back in Nutwood."

RUPERT'S PAL GETS CROSS

"Because your wretched dragon came
And stole food my one got the blame!"

Excitedly the dragon speaks
To Gregory in little squeaks.

"Mervyn," he says, "has just told me
Your dragon's hiding in a tree."

"I think," says Mr. Guineapig, "it's clear
That P.C. Growler should be here."

"The trouble was," Gregory goes on, "I didn't know how to get the right sort of food for Mervyn so he began to take leeks from anywhere he found them. I was too frightened to go to Constable Growler and tell him in case Mervyn got into bad trouble." At that Pong-Ping jumps up. "And my pet got into trouble instead of your Mervyn!" he bursts out. At the mention of Pong-Ping's dragon Mervyn sits up and begins to chatter excitedly to Gregory who seems to understand him.

When Mervyn has finished Gregory says, "When we were in Wales I learned to speak his language. Now he tells me that your dragon, Pong-Ping, came to find him and explain about the trouble it was in because of what Mervyn was doing. Now Mervyn says he's sorry and can he please go home." Mr. Guineapig puts on his coat. "I think we best get Constable Growler and explain," he says. "And you, Gregory, can find out from Mervyn where Pong-Ping can find his pet."

RUPERT SEES MERVYN OFF HOME

Says Growler when he's heard their tales,
"I think we'll send it back to Wales."

Then in comes Pong-Ping, smiling wide,
His little dragon by his side.

Next morning Mervyn's off again
To Nutchester to catch a train.

And so the dragon mystery ends
With everyone once more good friends.

Gregory's father returns with Constable Growler who looks very puzzled. Pong-Ping meanwhile has gone to fetch his pet dragon which Mervyn has said is hiding in a hollow tree near Gregory's house. Poor Growler can hardly believe his eyes when he is shown Mervyn. Then he hears about how Mervyn stowed away because he wanted to see the world and is sorry and wants to go home. "It's plain he meant no harm," he says, just as Pong-Ping bursts happily in with his own pet dragon.

So since everyone agrees that Mervyn meant no harm, it is decided to return him to Wales. And next morning the chums gather to say goodbye to him. "I shall take him to Nutchester on my bike," Growler tells him. "There he'll catch a train to Wales where I've arranged for someone to meet him." And so Mervyn sets off in a basket on the back of Constable Growler's bike, chattering happily at Gregory. "He says we're to come and visit *him* in Wales!" says the little guineapig. The End.

A Box For Your Paper Banger

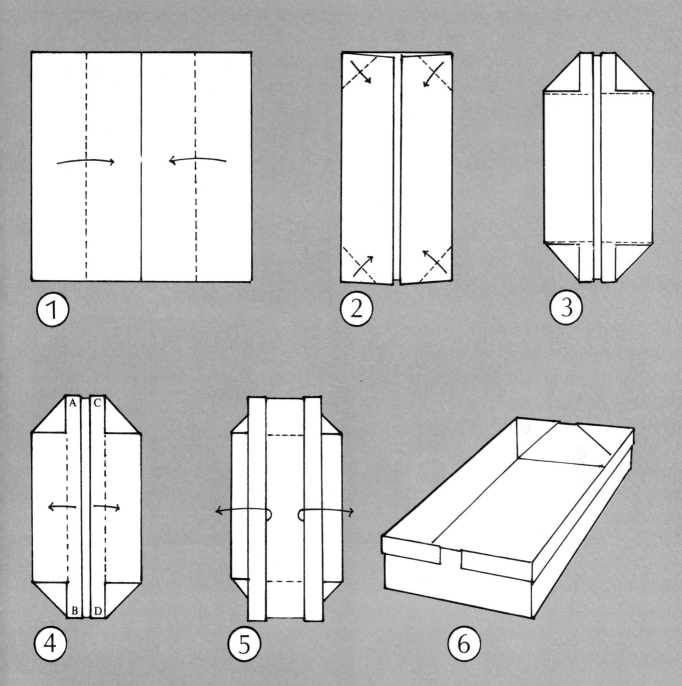

Although this is called A Box For Your Paper Banger you will find it useful in all sorts
of ways. Start with a square or rectangle of strong paper about the width of this page.
Typing paper is fine. Fold it edge to edge to get a centre line then fold the edges to the
centre along the dotted lines shown in (1). Fold down the four corners marked in (2).
Then fold top and bottom along the dotted lines in (3) to get a crease and unfold again.
Fold back the edges AB and CD along the dotted lines shown in (4). Then gently but
firmly open out as in (5) to give you the finished box (6).

RUPERT and

*"Oh, do, please, Mummy, say I may
Go to the Wise Old Goat's today."*

The Wise Old Goat has a nephew, Billy, and one morning Billy turns up at the Bears' house to ask if Rupert would like to join him in a hike to his uncle's castle in the hills. "I haven't seen him for ages," he says. "We can stay the night." "Oh, Mummy, may I?" Rupert begs. "Well, if you're sure Billy's uncle won't mind . . ." she says. And so later that day after a long walk from Nutwood, the chums reach the Wise Old Goat's castle.

the Mulp Gulper

So off they tramp across the fells
To where young Billy's uncle dwells.

"Hey, Uncle, I've brought Rupert Bear!"
But there's no one to answer there.

Billy hurries ahead to tell his uncle that he has brought Rupert. But there is no answer to his ring at the bell and only silence when he goes in and calls. "Maybe he's busy in his workshop," Rupert suggests. But when they search the house there is no sign of the Wise Old Goat. So they wait but still he doesn't come and at last they decide to go to bed. "He usually leaves a note if he's away for any time," Billy muses.

They wait but no one comes and so
The pals decide to bed they'll go.

John. Harrold.

RUPERT IS CHASED BY A BIRD

When still he's not come back next day
The pals decide they must not stay.

They've hardly set off down the track
Before a great bird turns them back.

The two turn tail and fairly scorch
Back to the shelter of the porch.

Then back and forth the great bird flies.
"It's 'saying' something!" Rupert cries.

Rupert and Billy hoped when they fell asleep that the Wise Old Goat might be back when they wakened. But no. And now they are really worried. "I don't like this," Rupert says. "I vote we go straight back to Nutwood for help." So as soon as they have had a bite to eat the two pals set out for home.

They haven't gone far, though, when a shadow falls over them. A great bird is just overhead. And as they try to walk on it swoops angrily.

"Run for it!" shouts Rupert. But their attempt to dash down the path back to Nutwood only makes the great bird swoop lower and squawk more angrily. So they turn and dash for the shelter of the castle doorway. Then the bird does something very strange. While the pals look on from the safety of the rocks near the door, it flies towards the mountains, returns and repeats the performance several times. "I don't think it was attacking us," Rupert says. "It's been trying to tell us something!"

RUPERT FOLLOWS THE BIRD

Then on the sill it comes to sit.
It wants the chums to follow it.

They send a note, their folk to tell,
What's going on and that they're well.

The bird returns and they set out
Still wondering what it's all about.

"This stream supplies our river, though
I must say, it seems rather low."

Rupert and Billy wave at the bird to show that they understand it wants to tell them something. Then they go back into the house where the bird appears and settles on a window sill. "Wait! I know you!" exclaims Billy. "You're my uncle's messenger bird!" The bird nods. "And you want us to go with you, right?" Rupert asks. Again a nod. That does it. In a moment Rupert is giving the bird a note to take to their parents to say what's happening, while Billy makes sandwiches.

It doesn't take the bird long to get back from Nutwood and Billy and Rupert are waiting, their knapsacks packed with food for the journey ahead.

At once the bird turns towards the mountains and the chums follow. Higher and higher it leads them until they reach a stream. "I know this," says Billy. "It's the stream that feeds our own Nutwood River. But I'm sure it was bigger last time I saw it." Now the bird turns upstream. It seems anxious to press on.

RUPERT FINDS THE SPRING DRY

It seems the spring is running dry.
This level should be much more high.

At last the bird stops where the spring
Just wets the rocks, a feeble thing.

It wants them to go in the cave.
Now neither of them feels so brave.

The bird makes such a fuss that though
They're frightened they just have to go.

The bird leads them higher into the mountains to a little lake which Billy calls a tarn. "It feeds the stream we've been following," he explains. "But it's very low." "Where does its water come from?" Rupert asks. "From a spring that starts higher up," Billy tells him. And that, it turns out, is where the bird is taking them. The water coming from the spring is a mere trickle and when at last they reach the cave where it starts there is hardly any water at all.

But the bird does not fly on. It perches on a rock outside the cave. "Well, what now?" Rupert asks. For answer the bird flaps its great wings and flies into the cave. The pals look at each other. And their looks say that they don't much fancy the idea of following it. But the bird won't have that. When it finds that it isn't being followed it emerges from the cave with a great squawk and sweeps into the gloom once more. "I–I suppose we'd better go in," quavers Rupert.

RUPERT'S OLD FRIEND IS FOUND

It hovers near a pile of rocks.
It flaps its wings and how it squawks!

They wonder what they're going to find,
Approach the rocks and peer behind.

The Wise Old Goat! He stirs. He moans.
"Oh, dear!" My poor old head!" he groans.

While checking on the spring he fell.
The bird was with him – just as well!

Inside the cave Rupert and Billy wait for their eyes to get used to the gloom. When they can see they are not much happier. The cave seems to go deep into the mountain. They can see traces of the spring which has stopped running now. Then they jump as the messenger bird which is hovering above a boulder squawks loudly. "It's showing us something," Rupert whispers. Very cautiously he leads the way to the boulder and peers behind it. "Look at this!" he gasps.

Lying behind the boulder is the Wise Old Goat! "Oh, uncle, what's happened?" Billy cries. At the sound of Billy's voice his uncle stirs. "Oh, my head!" he moans. The pals help him to sit up and Rupert produces his water bottle. The Wise Old Goat drinks from it. "That's better," he sighs. Then he tells the pals how he came up to see why the stream was drying up, saw that the spring had stopped, entered the cave, slipped on a rock and banged his head. Luckily the bird was with him.

RUPERT HAS A PLAN

Before he fell he saw something
Had been done to divert the spring.

They go to look, and, sure enough,
They find that someone's built a trough.

"Let's turn it back and maybe then
They'll come to change it round again."

They settle down their watch to keep.
But no one comes. They fall asleep.

Seeing its master safe the bird flies off again leaving him with the pals. "Just before I fell," says the Wise Old Goat, "I spied something strange. The spring had not actually dried up – look!" He points into the cave where the chums can just make out a sort of structure. They go closer to find the spring gushing freely into a wooden trough which disappears into the cave. Rupert gasps: "Someone has changed the way it goes!" "But who?" Billy whispers nervously.

"Whoever it was went to a lot of trouble to do it," says Billy's uncle. "But why?" Then Rupert has one of his ideas: "If they want it so much they'd be bound to come and see what's wrong if we change the direction of the stream back again." "Good idea" agrees the Wise Old Goat, and within a few minutes the chums have turned part of the trough so that the spring once more flows out of the cave. Then by the light of the Goat's pocket lantern they settle to wait.

RUPERT FINDS A NOTE

He starts awake but not before
The spring has been turned round once more!

When they get up to look they find
Someone has left a note behind.

"We need the water," says the note.
"And we do!" says the Wise Old Goat.

Again they turn the water round.
But leave a message to be found.

Well, the three friends wait and wait and try hard to stay awake. But nothing happens and, of course, they fall asleep.

Suddenly Rupert is awake. What was that? Like scurrying feet disappearing into the depths of the cave? By the dim light of the lantern he looks around. Next moment the others start up at his cry – "The spring! It's been switched back again!" When the friends scramble to their feet and go to look, Rupert spots something on a rock.

"Look! A note!" he cries. "It says, 'Please do not take back your water. We need it very badly'." "They seem friendly," says Billy. But his uncle look solemn. "We must have the water, too," he says. "Without it the river in Nutwood would dry up. We must switch it back." But while the chums are yet again changing the direction of the spring, he writes a reply on the back of the note: "Sorry, we must have spring too. But we want to help you. Tell us how."

The plan is they'll pretend to sleep.
In fact, a careful watch they'll keep.

They doze off and when they come round
They find they're pinioned to the ground.

"We've found your note and now we see
You're friendly so we'll set you free."

From far away there comes a roar.
They rush to turn the spring once more.

Now the Wise Old Goat explains his plan to the chums. He will leave his note where it will be found when the mysterious strangers come back to find out why the spring has been switched once again: "We shall pretend to be asleep." But although the three lie very still, just now and then opening an eye to see what is happening, nothing stirs and they fall asleep.

They waken to a shock. They are tied to the ground by strong cords. And someone's coming!

Fearfully the friends listen to the approaching footsteps. But although the figures who appear from the depths of the cave are among the oddest Rupert has seen, they look friendly. Their leader addresses Rupert: "Sorry we tied you up. We didn't know what you might do . . . but now we've seen your note." Meanwhile his companions are untying the three friends. Suddenly – an angry roar from deep in the cave. Immediately the little creatures rush towards the spring.

RUPERT HEARS AN AWFUL NOISE

Until the trough's been turned around
The rocks with angry roars resound.

"Mulp Gulper is a creature who'll
Burn down our homes if not kept cool."

The Wise Old Goat says, "If we may,
Let's see this creature. Lead the way!"

"We're Spelies . . ." starts the little guide.
A strange noise halts them in full stride.

Looking terrified, the little creatures heave round the trough under the spring so that once more the water runs into the cave. Soon the roaring sinks to a rumble, then silence. The one who seems to be the leader apologises: "I really am sorry. I knew this would happen if we couldn't have the spring water . . ." "But what made that noise?" asks the Wise Old Goat. "The Mulp Gulper," comes the reply. "If the mulps aren't kept cool it may burn down our homes! If it weren't for the wretched creature we shouldn't need the spring water." The Wise Old Goat nods. "If we're to help you I think we should see this Mulp Gulper," he says. "Very well," says the other and, switching on the lamp on his head, turns back into the cave. "We are the Spelies," he explains as they go. "The caves are our homes. Well, some time ago the Mulp Gulper came . . ." Just then the friends hear a greedy, slurping, guzzling sound from somewhere not far ahead of them.

RUPERT SEES THE MULP GULPER

Then forward to the edge they creep,
And down into a cavern peep.

And there's Mulp Gulper, great fat brute!
Devouring piles of soaking fruit.

They're wrong-way plums the dragon gulps,
And known, the Spelie says, as mulps.

"If not kept cool that beast breathes fire.
What happens – look! – is really dire!"

The sound grows as the cave gets wider and lighter. Ahead, Rupert and the others can make out a big well-lit cavern with the doors of little homes let into its walls. The Spelie stops them, steals forward and peers over into the cavern. Then he beckons to the friends. "There," he points, "is the Mulp Gulper, gulping mulps as fast as we can pick them." And there below is a fat dragon with, before it, a great pile of fruit being soaked by spring water from the trough.

"Are those plums?" whispers Rupert. "Sort of," says the Spelie. "But they grow the wrong way round – down into the earth." Below, Spelies are dumping barrowloads of the fruit in front of the dragon. "It dotes on them and we can't get rid of it," says the Spelie. "What's worse is that it's a fire-breathing dragon and the mulps have to be soaked to keep its insides cool or it breathes fire . . ." He points to a scorched doorway.

"I've an idea," says the Wise Old Goat.

78

RUPERT TASTES A MULP

Each tries a mulp. The test is brief!
The taste is foul beyond belief!

The Wise Old Goat says, "Now, you two,
I have a little job for you."

"Go to my workshop, that's your task,
And bring back here a special flask."

The stream before was hardly high.
But now, they see, it's almost dry.

The Wise Old Goat whispers to the Spelie leader who, a moment later, hands a mulp to each of the three friends. "Try them," says the Wise Old Goat and nods to the chums. All three bite into the fruit and . . . "Ugh!" they chorus, spitting out what they've bitten off. "I've never tasted anything so awful!" gasps Rupert as he and Billy wash away the taste with mouthfuls of spring water. The Wise Old Goat meanwhile is smiling and writing busily in his notebook.

When the Wise Old Goat has finished writing he says to Rupert and Billy, "I want you to fetch something from my workshop. This will tell you how to find it." He hands Rupert a page from his notebook. A few minutes later the friends are on their way out of the cave. On their way to the Wise Old Goat's home they pass the tarn. By now it is almost empty. "We must hurry if Nutwood river isn't to dry up altogether," says Rupert. On they go by the stream, now a mere trickle.

RUPERT IS SENT ON AN ERRAND

At last they reach the castle where
They hurry to the workshop there.

"Yes, it's the right one, I can tell.
I say, what's that delightful smell?"

The Wise Old Goat is waiting when
The two pals reach the cave again.

Fixed to a branch beside the trough
He's rigged a bag of porous stuff.

Rupert and Billy make straight for the workshop when they reach the Wise Old Goat's home. Rupert studies the note he has been given. "The cupboard in the corner," he reads. "That's it." he points. When the pals open it there is such a lovely smell. They sniff happily. "Now the round flask from the top shelf," Rupert reads. "Yes, here it is." He lifts it down carefully. "Now let's get some bread and cheese and hurry back to the cave," he tells Billy.

And so Rupert and Billy start the long haul back to the cave, carrying the flask between them. "What do you think it is?" Billy asks. "I can't imagine," Rupert says. "But everything in that cupboard had the loveliest smell."

The Wise Old Goat is waiting for them and leads them into the cave. He has been busy while they've been gone. He has fixed a branch to the trough and from it hung a fine mesh bag. "Good, you've brought the right stuff," he says.

RUPERT IS PUZZLED

They see the contents emptied out
And wonder what it's all about.

The drops ooze through, a moment cling,
Then drop into the rushing spring.

And now, they're told, they wait, but not
How long they must, nor yet for what.

Then suddenly that awful roar,
But much worse than it was before.

The chums still have no idea of how the Wise Old Goat means to get rid of the Mulp Gulper and he is not offering any clues. Smiling, he takes the flask and opens it. The smell is quite delicious. Then he empties the contents into the mesh bag over the trough. For a while nothing happens then slowly globules of thick golden liquid drip from the bag into the swiftly-flowing water. Rupert watches, fascinated. The smell is one of the nicest he has ever come across.

"Now," says the Wise Old Goat, "we sit and wait". "Wait for what?" Rupert asks as the others settle themselves on the rocks. But Billy's uncle only smiles his gentle mysterious smile.

Then when Rupert thinks he can't stand not knowing for another moment, there comes a great, echoing roar of rage from the cavern where the Mulp Gulper is. Everyone jumps – except the Wise Old Goat. "Ah, that is exactly what I hoped for," he says with a smile.

RUPERT SEES THE GULPER FLEE

There is – as to the noise they race –
A smile upon the Wise Goat's face.

The mulps it so enjoyed before
It spits out with disgusted roar.

It grabs its tum. It's plain to tell
Mulp Gulper does feel most unwell.

"It won't eat mulps again. Don't fear,
You'll never see that brute back here!"

"Oh dear, something's upset the wretched beast!" says the Spelies' leader. "We must see what's happened!" And he leads the rush back to the cavern. Rupert, Billy and the Wise Old Goat hurry after them. The two pals are alarmed. But not Billy's uncle.

When at last they look down into the cavern they can hardly believe their eyes. The dragon is still gulping great mouthfuls of mulps, but as fast as it does it spits them out again with a roar of disgust.

"The water's still running on the mulps, so that can't have upset it," Rupert says. "But that is exactly what *has* upset it," counters the Wise Old Goat. And before he can say anything more, the Mulp Gulper, looking extremely unhappy, clutches its fat tummy, gives a long, low moan and dashes out of the cavern. The Spelies burst into cheers and the Wise Old Goat says, "I'm quite sure it will never fancy mulps again and that you will never see it back here."

82

RUPERT TASTES THE MIXTURE

The Wise Old Goat's the hero now!
Just hear the Spelies' happy row!

"That stuff," says Rupert, "must taste grim!"
"Then try it," his friend urges him.

"Well, though it made the Gulper sick,
I can at least try one small lick."

He dips it. Licks it. But – what's this?
The taste is lovely – super – bliss!

The Spelies surround the Wise Old Goat, cheering and wishing they were big enough to pat him on the back. But he shakes his head and says, "No time to waste. We must turn the spring or the Nutwood river will dry up." As the Spelies rush to do this Rupert points to the bag over the trough. "That's the stuff that got rid of the Mulp Gulper, isn't it?" The Wise Old Goat nods. "Then we'd better not have it in our water," says Rupert. "Why not?" smiles his old friend.

"Why not?" repeats Rupert. "I should have said that was plain. The Mulp Gulper was enjoying his mulps until that stuff got on them. Then look what happened to him." "Come here," says the Wise Old Goat. "Now dip your finger into the bag and taste it." Very cautiously Rupert does as he's asked. The stuff in the bag feels a bit like honey when you stick your finger in it (which you shouldn't). Even more cautiously Rupert licks his finger. "Oooh! Lovely!" he breathes.

RUPERT HEARS HOW IT WORKED

"Because it loved the mulps, I knew
The Gulper would detest this brew."

The Spelies shout as our three go,
"When you need help just let us know!"

And now the spring is flowing free,
That's more like how the tarn should be.

"Most odd. The river fell and then
Quite suddenly filled up again!"

Now the Wise Old Goat explains: "The stuff we put in the water is my invention – a mixture of the loveliest tastes you can imagine. I saw that any creature that liked the mulp's awful taste would find this mixture sickening and hateful. I was right!"

Later when the three friends set off for home the Spelies come out of their cave to cheer them on their way. "Any time we can help you let us know and we'll do it!" their leader calls.

When Rupert and the others reach the tarn the little mountain lake is beginning to fill nicely, and the stream from it is running swiftly again down to Nutwood and its river.

At supper time that night Mr. Bear tells Rupert: "Strange thing happened today. The water in the river dropped badly. We were frightened it would dry up altogether. Suddenly it has started to fill again. Odd, isn't it?" "Just wait 'til they hear the full story," Rupert thinks. The End.

Your Own Rupert Story

*Title:*_____

Why not try colouring the pictures below and writing a story to fit them?
Write your story in four parts, one for each picture, saying what it shows.
Then, faintly in pencil, print each part neatly on the lines under its
picture. When they fit, go over the printing with a ball-pen. There is
space at the top for a title.

"It's really hot. I think I'll take
A dip since I'm so near the lake."

Phew! It *is* hot! And Rupert is beginning to feel that this isn't really the sort of weather for a ramble on the common. Then he spots the lake below and suddenly a dip in it seems very attractive. So down he goes and he has just got there when he hears a splash. Someone else with the same idea, he thinks. But, no! The splash is followed by a cry for help. Rupert dashes towards the sound of more splashing.

he ICEBERG

A cry! A splash! An awful din!
"My goodness! Someone's fallen in!"

"I'm coming!" Rupert gives a shout,
And finds an old man climbing out.

On a stretch of bank shaded by a big tree he finds an old man with a long beard trying to climb out of the water. With Rupert's help the old man scrambles ashore. "Are you all right?" Rupert asks anxiously. "Yes, apart from being soaked," the man replies. "I foolishly leant over too far with my net . . . and, ah, yes, there it is. Would you be a good little bear and get it ashore for me? I should hate to lose it."

Although the old man's sopping wet,
He's more concerned about his net.

"Oh, please," the old man begs, "be quick!"
So Rupert gets it with a stick.

"I'll throw the weeds out," Rupert cries.
"No! Don't do that!" the man replies.

"Now, come along and you shall see
Why those weeds mean so much to me."

And in his house the old man shows
Tanks full of water plants in rows.

Wondering why the old man is so concerned about a fishing net when he is standing there soaked to the skin, Rupert gets a stick and manages to pull the net to the bank. The old man is delighted and Rupert is very curious to see what the net holds that can affect him like this. But it has only water-weeds in it. "I'll tip these back," he says. "No, no!" cries the old man. "I want them. Those weeds are what I was fishing for when I fell in."

Then the old man sees the look on Rupert's face and chuckles: "I can see you don't understand. Well, if you care to follow me to my house –" He points to a mansion on the far shore. "– I shall explain." And off he scampers at a surprising rate with Rupert at his heels.

In the mansion he leads the way to a room lined with glass tanks. "Stay here and have a look," he invites Rupert. "I'm going off to change." The tanks, Rupert sees, are full of water plants.

RUPERT GETS AN INVITATION

*"I'm flying to the far North where
A seaweed grows that's very rare."*

*"And, if you like, you may come, too.
Go home and ask. I'll wait for you."*

*Though it's still very hot next day,
With coat and scarf he's on his way.*

*"So glad you're coming, little bear.
We're going in my seaplane there."*

"Now," the old man says when he returns, "you see why I didn't want those weeds thrown back. I am a collector of water plants and I have almost every kind." It seems an odd thing to collect but Rupert politely looks interested and the old man goes on about his hobby over tea and later as he walks back part of the way with Rupert. "I'm going north tomorrow to look for a very rare plant," he says. "You may care to come too?" "Ooh, yes!" says Rupert.

So Rupert and the old man agree to meet next day near what looks like a huge boat-house. "And bring warm clothes," the old man says.

"It must be very far north if you need warm clothes at this time of year," says Mrs. Bear. But she agrees to his going, and off he sets next day carrying coat and scarf. When he gets to where they are to meet he finds the old man in flying gear, and, out on the lake, a big seaplane. "We are taking my aircraft," the old man says.

They climb aboard. The engines roar.
Then off towards the North they soar.

High over northern seas they go,
And there's the place they want, below.

The man says, "This takes time, I've found.
So why don't you just look around?"

He wonders, looking out to sea,
"Whatever can those white rocks be?"

"So this is what was in that huge boat-shed," Rupert thinks as he climbs aboard the seaplane. The old man must be very well-off to be able to afford such a machine. Then the engines burst into life, the seaplane skims over the lake and a minute later they are high over Nutwood, heading north. Soon the summery countryside is far behind and they are over a cold-looking sea. By the time they reach where they're going Rupert is glad he brought coat and scarf.

It is a bleak, rocky place where the pair come ashore. "Now, this weed-hunting can take a bit of time," the old man says. "So, why don't you do a bit of scrambling about and exploring to keep yourself warm?" That seems a good idea and off goes Rupert, promising to be careful. He likes climbing and makes his way to the top of a little headland. And there, out to sea, he sees something he has never seen before. "What lovely white rocks those are!" he marvels.

RUPERT MEETS SAILOR SAM

Then Rupert hears a cheery shout,
And from a hut a tar comes out.

"Rocks, you say?" he laughs. "That's droll!"
They're icebergs! See, we're near the Pole."

"Then Uncle Polar must live near.
Look, that's him in this snapshot here."

The sailor – name of Sam – says, "We
Can take the boat I've here with me."

Suddenly Rupert finds himself being hailed from somewhere below. He climbs down a little way, and there is a motor-boat, a hut and an old-fashioned sailor – the sort who used to be called Jack Tar. This one, though, turns out to be called Sailor Sam who has been fishing. Well, of course, the first thing Rupert asks about is the "white rocks". "Rocks?" cries Sam. "They're not rocks! They're icebergs! We're not so far from the North Pole here." The North Pole! The words have

Rupert searching his pockets. Yes, here it is! He produces a snapshot and shows it to Sam. "My Uncle Polar Bear!" he says. "He sent me this picture at Christmas. He lives near the Pole." "Then why don't we visit him?" laughs Sam. "My boat's a fast little craft. We could be there and back in no time!" "Oh, could we?" Rupert cries. "I'd love to!" And so, with Sam's promise to get him back in good time, Rupert scrambles down to the boat.

"It shouldn't be too long a run,"
Says Sam. And Rupert thinks, "What fun!"

Now more and more icebergs appear
As even further north they steer.

Says Sam, "Now off you go and find
Your uncle. I shall stay behind."

"Oh, please," he asks, "do you know where
I may find Mr. Polar Bear?"

Sam holds the boat steady while Rupert climbs into it. "It's not much to look at," he says. "But it's sturdy and nippy, as you'll see." Sure enough, the little boat cuts through the water at a cracking pace. "This is fun!" Rupert laughs, and Sam agrees, for it's pretty boring just fishing by yourself day after day and the trip makes a pleasant break. As they near their destination the icebergs get more and more numerous. "I should hate to hit one," says Rupert.

At last Sam stops and moors on an ice-bound shore. "Now, off you go and find your uncle," he tells Rupert. "Take this compass to help you find your way back. I'll stay here and fish." Of course, Rupert doesn't know exactly where his uncle lives but guesses that the local creatures will, and so he stops and asks some puffins, "Please, can you tell me where Mr. Polar Bear lives?" A sea-swallow who overhears this pipes up, "Yes, I know where. Come on, I'll show you."

A friendly sea-bird leads him to
His Uncle Polar Bear's igloo.

There's not a sign of life to see,
But on he trudges cheerfully.

When he arrives he gives a shout
And Uncle Polar Bear pops out.

His uncle can't believe his eyes.
"But how did you get here?" he cries.

They don't have to go far before the sea-swallow stops and says, "There!" Rupert looks over the barren white landscape. "Where?" he asks. "There!" says the bird and indicates what looks like a mound of snow. So Rupert thanks the bird and sets off for the mound. There's not a sign of life to be seen but Rupert trudges on cheerfully and as he gets close, he thinks, "Of course, it's an igloo sort of thing. I suppose I was expecting a house something like ours."

Unlike the usual sort of igloo this one doesn't have any sort of entrance. So Rupert has to stand outside and shout, "Uncle!" He jumps when a hole is punched in the snow wall and a large head appears. "Good gracious!" it says. Then more snow is kicked out to make a doorway of sorts and out steps Uncle Polar Bear. "Rupert!" he cries. "What a lovely surprise. Now come inside at once and tell me how on earth you come to be here." Inside there is only a bed and a stove.

*"Our winter lasts for half a year.
You could be trapped that long up here."*

*"If that is so, I mustn't stay.
I only came out for the day."*

*"Then off you go now!" Uncle cries
"Or night will catch you by surprise."*

*So Rupert, waving, turns to go.
His tracks are still plain in the snow.*

Uncle Polar rustles up a hot drink for Rupert and then he says something strange: "I suppose you have brought your bed." "Bed?" repeats Rupert. "But why should I?" And then he learns something which alarms him. "Well, winter lasts for months up here," his uncle says. "It's dark all the time so we sleep right through it . . . and it's almost on us now." He points to the disappearing sun. "Oh, dear, I'm only here for the day!" Rupert cries. "I must be off at once!"

Of course, Uncle Polar is sorry Rupert can't stay longer. But he quite understands. "Now, hurry," he says, "or you may be caught by the long winter night. You must visit me again some other time – but not at this time of year."

So Rupert says goodbye to Uncle Polar, promises to give his best wishes to Mr. and Mrs. Bear, and sets off back to Sam and the boat. "It shouldn't take long," he tells himself. "All I need do is follow the tracks I made coming here."

RUPERT LOSES THE COMPASS

But now as snow begins to fall,
He cannot see his tracks at all.

He shouts, and to his great delight,
He hears Sam calling, "You're all right!"

But Rupert's lost – and this is grim –
The compass that Sam lent to him.

By now the snowstorm's so severe
That Sam decides they can't stay here.

But it is not to be as easy as that. Rupert has not been going long when a strong wind rises and it begins to snow. In no time his tracks vanish. This is frightening. Nothing but a whirling whiteness all around him. Gamely he plods on, but he has no way of knowing if he is going the right way. How awful it would be to get lost out here with the long winter night coming on! The thought so frightens him that he shouts, "Sam! Help!" And a great wave of relief sweeps over him when Sam's voice calls back, "You're all right!"

When Sam hears what Uncle Polar has said about the winter night starting he says, "Then we best be off now. Just let me have the compass I lent you." Rupert reaches into his pocket. No compass! "I've lost it!" he wails. "Then we must take our chances," Sam declares. "Anything's better than being trapped here all winter." So the two scramble into the boat and head into the storm.

RUPERT IS WRECKED

They battle on through raging seas.
As darkness falls the two friends freeze.

A sudden crash! And Rupert squeals
As both are flung head over heels.

They aren't hurt, but nonetheless,
Poor Sam's boat is an awful mess!

When the storm dies they see the boat,
As it is now, could never float.

The storm rises, the seas get rougher and the wind drives the snow ever more fiercely against Rupert and Sam. As near as he can tell, Sam holds his course, and though it gets darker and darker he does not slacken speed. It is too important to get well away from the land of the long night. Rupert is thinking how lucky it is that the boat is such a sturdy one when – Crrrash! The front of the boat seems to explode and the two friends are pitched head over heels!

What Rupert feared earlier has happened. They have struck an iceberg. Luckily neither is hurt and they huddle into what shelter they can find, waiting for the storm to blow itself out. When at last it passes, and its darkness with it, Rupert and Sam survey the damage. It's terrible. Only the back part of the little craft has survived. The front half is smashed beyond repair – fit only for firewood. It is plain that the brave little boat's days are over.

RUPERT HAS A BRAINWAVE

Now Sam slumps down in deep despair.
But Rupert says, "The rudder's there."

So to the ice the boat they rope.
And now at least they have a hope.

"The engine works!" Sam shouts with glee.
"The iceberg's now our boat, you see!"

It's clumsy and it's very slow.
But, still, towards the South they go.

It's all too much for Sam and he slumps down in despair. Then Rupert who has been examining what's left of the boat says, "Sam, the rudder and the propeller are perfectly all right . . . I've got an idea if they can be made to work. Do we have any rope?" "Yes," says Sam, "But what . . .?" "Then help me to get the stern back into the water and we'll lash the boat to the iceberg." Sam's face lights up as he gets the idea. And in no time the pair are working busily.

At last they are ready. Will the engine work? They hold their breath as Sam works the starter. Oh, great! The engine bursts into life. Now the whole iceberg is their boat. A slow, clumsy boat. But it is moving, that's what is important. And with Sam holding the rudder lines and steering by sun and stars, it is moving in the right direction, away from the dangerous Polar seas and the long, long night. Rupert sits on the peak of the iceberg acting as lookout.

RUPERT IS REALLY WORRIED

Just as they think the worst is past
They find the iceberg's melting fast.

And then the engine loses speed!
Somehow it's got all choked with weed.

Sam says, "We're done for now, I fear.
The ice won't last much longer here."

Despairingly he tries again . . .
But look! Yes, it's the old man's 'plane!

As the strange iceberg-craft moves slowly south the two friends notice something they might have expected. As the air gets warmer the iceberg is melting. Can they reach land before it melts away altogether? There's nothing for it but to keep going. Then when the iceberg is no more than a quarter of its old size, the engine stops and Sam can't re-start it. When he scrambles to the stern and looks he sees why. The propeller is entangled in thick seaweed.

Desperately he tries to clear the weed. But after what seems ages he has managed to free only a few strands. "Oh, Sam, the iceberg will melt in half an hour!" Rupert groans. "Then I think we are done for," says Sam. "I can't move the rest of the stuff in that time." But he keeps trying, though with almost no success. Suddenly Rupert's sharp ears pick up a droning. He gazes skywards. He can hardly believe his eyes. "Sam!" he yells. "It's the old man's seaplane!"

RUPERT IS RESCUED

The old man spots the boat, descends
And taxies over to the friends.

And as he throws the pair a rope,
He says, "I almost gave up hope."

To what Sam says he pays no heed.
His eyes are fastened on the weed.

"Oh, my!," he gasps. "This weed you caught
Is just the very thing I sought!"

The old man has spotted Rupert's wildly waving scarf and eases the big seaplane down on to the water. Gently he taxies over to the iceberg-craft so as not to swamp it. He climbs from the cockpit with a length of rope which he ties to one of the float struts before throwing the other end to Sam. Then when the seaplane is close enough he jumps on to the rapidly melting iceberg. "What on earth happened to you?" he asks Rupert. "I'd almost given up hope of seeing you again!"

Sam starts to tell about how he took Rupert to see his uncle and agrees that they ought to have told the old man first . . . Then he stops. For the old man isn't listening to him. His eyes are fastened on the seaweed that Sam is still clutching. He takes it from Sam's hand and gazes at it. The other two look at each other and wonder what's happening. Then the old man speaks: "This is amazing! The very seaweed I flew north to find. I found none. But *you* have!"

RUPERT GOES HOME

"Now, Sam," he says, "I'll bear the cost
Of making good the boat you've lost."

As they take off and start to climb.
The wreck sinks. They were just in time!

It's so nice to be home again,
With Daddy there to meet the 'plane.

And finally the old man gives
Our Sam the shack where he still lives!

The old man could not be more delighted. "Oh, well," says Sam, "thank goodness someone has got something out of this sorry business." And he gazes at the remains of his boat. "My dear sir," cries the old man. "You must not suffer by this adventure which has ended so well for me. I shall pay for a new boat for you!" Then he looks about him at the dwindling iceberg. "But I think we should be going right now." So they climb into the seaplane and go – not a moment too soon!

Mr. Bear is waiting anxiously when Rupert and the others return. "My goodness, you had us worried," he says. "Me too," laughs the old man.

Now everything is fine . . . except that Sailor Sam, it turns out, has no home to go to. "Then I have just the place for you!" cries the old man. And he leads the way to a roomy, well-built shack on his estate. Sam is speechless with delight. So is Rupert who has come to like Sam. And to this day he often has tea at Sam's place. THE END.